KU-150-168

for Katy and Anna

Text copyright © 2001 by Paul Stewart. Illustrations copyright © 2001 by Chris Riddell.
The rights of Paul Stewart and Chris Riddell to be identified as the author and illustrator
of this work have been asserted by them in accordance with the Copyright, Designs and Patents Act, 1988.
First published in Great Britain in 2001 by Andersen Press Ltd., 20 Vauxhall Bridge Road, London SW1V 2SA.
This paperback edition first published in 2002 by Andersen Press.
Published in Australia by Random House Australia Pty., 20 Alfred Street, Milsons Point, Sydney, NSW 2061.
All rights reserved.
Colour separated in Italy by Fotoriproduzione Grafiche, Verona.
Printed and bound in Italy by Grafiche AZ, Verona.

10   9   8   7   6   5   4   3   2   1

British Library Cataloguing in Publication Data available.

ISBN 1 84270 089 8

This book has been printed on acid-free paper

Rabbit's Wish

HACKNEY LIBRARY SERVICES

THIS BOOK MUST BE RETURNED TO THE LIBRARY ON OR
BEFORE THE LAST DATE STAMPED. FINES MAY BE
CHARGED IF IT IS LATE. AVOID FINES BY RENEWING THE
BOOK BY TELEPHONE, POST OR PERSONAL VISIT
(SUBJECT TO IT NOT BEING RESERVED).

PEOPLE WHO ARE OVER 60, UNDER 17 OR REGISTERED
DISABLED ARE NOT CHARGED FINES.   PS.6578(E&L)

CLAPTON LIBRARY
Northwold Road
London E5 8RA
Tel: 020 8356 2570
Fax: 020 8806 7848

1 0 OCT 2003   1 0 NOV 2003

- 9 JUN 2004

1 7 AUG 2005   2 0 AUG 2004

- 8 FEB 2005

- 9 FEB 2006   1 0 MAY 2005

- 9 FEB 2006

- 1 MAR 2008   1 1 APR 2006

1 8 NOV 2010   7 FEB 2007

1 2 MAY 2007

1 7 MAR 2011   7 MAR 2008

2 0 DEC 2010

- 2 FEB 2011

LONDON BOROUGH OF HACKNEY

3 8040 01150 1493

Rabbit's Wish

by Paul Stewart
with pictures by Chris Riddell

LONDON BOROUGH OF
HACKNEY
LIBRARY SERVICES

LOCAT	C L A
ACC. NO.	
CLASS	

Ⓐ

Andersen Press
London

"Look at the sky, Hedgehog," said Rabbit.
"It's all beautiful and red."
"I like it better when it's twinkly and black,"
said Hedgehog. "Besides, you know what they say
about red skies."
"Remind me," said Rabbit.
"Red sky in the morning, shepherd's warning,"
said Hedgehog. "Rain is on its way."

Hedgehog yawned. "Time for me to go to bed," he said.
"So soon?" said Rabbit.
"Yes, Rabbit," said Hedgehog. "You are a day creature
and I am a night creature. That is the way it is."
Rabbit nodded sadly. "Night-night, Hedgehog.
I mean, *day-day!*"

As Hedgehog disappeared from view,
Rabbit sighed a great big, lonely sigh.
"I wish," he said, "that just for once,
Hedgehog could stay up all day with me."

With his friend gone, Rabbit did what he always did. He had breakfast.

A little grass.

A dandelion leaf . . .

Suddenly – *plop* – a raindrop landed on his nose.

"Bother!" said Rabbit. "Hedgehog was right.
Rain was on its way. And now it's here!"

As Rabbit hopped back to his burrow, the rain grew heavier and heavier. "How wet it is!" he said.

Rabbit shook the water from his fur,
wiped the mud from his paws,
and scampered underground.

"My burrow," said Rabbit happily. "So warm.
So cosy. So *dry!*" He frowned. "But it is also rather
messy," he said. "As it is raining *out*side, I will stay
*in*side and tidy up."

Rabbit busied himself all morning.

He swept the floor.

He made his bed.

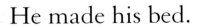

He sorted through his treasures,
one by one . . .

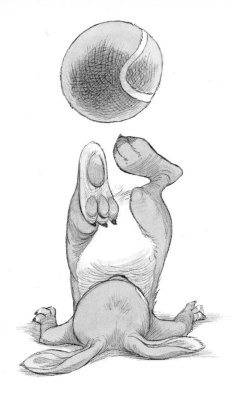  

The ball.   The string.   The woolly thing.

And most precious of all, the bottle of moonlight that Hedgehog had given him.

"Oh, Hedgehog, I *do* miss you," said Rabbit. "I . . ."

"Water!" Rabbit cried. "There's water in my burrow!"
The water was trickling down the tunnel and seeping up
through the floor. It quickly soaked Rabbit's bed of straw,
and set his treasures bobbing.

With the bottle of moonlight in one arm, and the ball,
the string and the woolly thing in the other,
Rabbit hurried from his burrow.

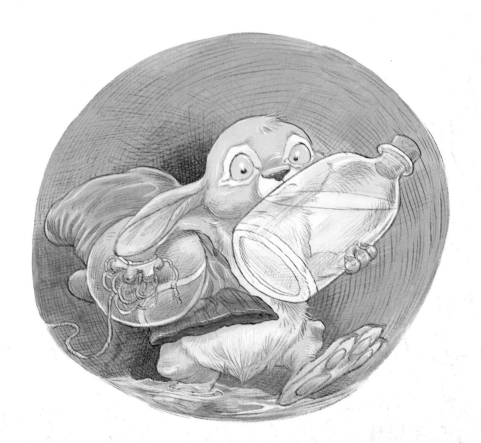

Rabbit couldn't believe his eyes.
The rain was heavier than ever.
And the lake! It was higher than he had seen it before –
so high that Rabbit's little hill had been turned into an island.

Far away, on the other side of the lake, the tops of Hedgehog's
bramble patch poked up above the swirling, muddy water.
Rabbit dropped his treasures. He ran this way and that.
"Hedgehog!" he cried. "Hedgehog, where are you?"

"Here I am," said a little voice.
Rabbit spun round. Hedgehog was standing down by
the water's edge.

"Hedgehog!" cried Rabbit.
"Rabbit!" cried Hedgehog.

"I was so *worried!*" said Rabbit.
"There was no need to be worried," said Hedgehog.
"I'm a good swimmer. When the water woke me,
I was worried about *you!* So I swam across the lake
to find you."

Rabbit stared at his friend with wide-open eyes.
"You're so brave!" he said. "But you mustn't catch cold."
He put the woolly thing on Hedgehog's head.

"But what are we going to do *now*, Hedgehog?" said Rabbit. "My burrow is full of water. Your bed is at the bottom of the lake. And it's *still* raining!"

"I know just what we can do," said Hedgehog. "We can play."

"Yes!" said Rabbit. "We can play together in the rain!"

They played catch.

They played tug-of-war.

They played boats.

The rain stopped, the sky cleared and the stars came out.
Rabbit and Hedgehog sat down at the edge of the lake.
"Hedgehog," said Rabbit. "I have a confession."
"What do you mean?" said Hedgehog.
"I have something to tell you," said Rabbit . . .

"It was my fault that everything happened.
I wished that you could stay up all day with me."
He looked down sorrowfully. "And my wish came true."
"I'm glad that it did," said Hedgehog. "Maybe next time
I will wish that you could stay up all night. With me!"
"I'd like that," said Rabbit. He yawned. "But now it's time
for *me* to go to bed."

"Night-night, Rabbit," said Hedgehog.
"Night-night, Hedgehog," said Rabbit.

Stories about Rabbit and Hedgehog

"Rabbit and Hedgehog are a winning pair."
Wendy Cope in the *Daily Telegraph*

A Little Bit of Winter
Hardback ISBN 0 86264 814 9
Paperback ISBN 0 86264 998 6

The Birthday Presents
Hardback ISBN 0 86264 892 0
Paperback ISBN 1 84270 035 9

Rabbit's Wish
Hardback ISBN 0 86264 719 3
Paperback ISBN 1 84270 089 8

What Do You Remember?
New in Hardback ISBN 1 84270 080 4
(JULY 2002)